THE BLIND GIRL

AN EROTIC ROMANCE

JADE'S EROTIC ADVENTURES
BOOK 55

VICTORIA RUSH

VOLUME 55

JADE'S EROTIC ADVENTURES - BOOK 55

COPYRIGHT

The Blind Girl © 2024 Victoria Rush

Cover Design © 2016 PhotoMaras

All Rights Reserved

ALSO BY VICTORIA RUSH

Adult Fairytales:

The Enchanted Forest: An Erotic Fairytale

The Land of Giants: An Erotic Fairytale

The Dragon's Lair: An Erotic Fairytale

Witch's Brew: An Erotic Fairytale

The Mage's Spell: An Erotic Fairytale

The Mermaid Lagoon: An Erotic Fairytale

The Coven: An Erotic Fairytale

Rapunzel: An Erotic Fairytale

The Seven Dwarfs: An Erotic Fairytale

The Land of Mutants: An Erotic Fairytale

The Erotic Temple: A Sexy Fairytale (Coming Soon)

Erotica Themed Bundles:

Voyeur: Lesbian Erotica Bundle

Public Affairs: A Lesbian Anthology

Futa Fantasies: The Ladyboy Collection

Threesomes: The Lesbian Collection

Threesomes - Volume 2: The Lesbian Collection

First Time: A Lesbian Anthology

Hedonism: An Erotic Anthology

Switch Hitters: Bisexual Erotica

Taboo Erotica: The Lesbian Series

BDSM: The Lesbian Collection

Party Games: The Erotic Collection

Party Games 2: The Erotic Collection

All Girl 1: Lesbian Erotica Bundle

All Girl 2: Lesbian Erotica Bundle

All Girl 3: Lesbian Erotica Bundle

All Girl 4: Lesbian Erotica Bundle

Erotic Fairytale Bundles:

Clover's Fantasy Adventures: Books 1 - 5

Clover's Fantasy Adventures: Books 6 - 10

Erotic Fantasy:

Pirate's Bounty: A Time Travel Adventure

Wild West: A Time Travel Adventure

Private Riley: A Time Travel Adventure

Cleopatra's Secret: A Time Travel Adventure

Bounty Hunter 2125: A Time Travel Adventure

Ninja Assassin: A Time Travel Adventure

The 300: A Time Travel Adventure

Arabian Nights: An Erotic Fairytale (coming soon...)

Steamy Time Travel Bundles:

Riley's Time Travel Adventures: Books 1 - 5

Lesbian Erotica:

The Dinner Party: Lesbian Voyeur Erotica

The Darkroom: Bisexual Voyeur Erotica

Naked Yoga: Lesbian Transgender Erotica

Nude Cruise: Bisexual Voyeur Erotica

Rush Hour: Taboo Public Sex

The Girl Next Door: First Time Lesbian Erotic Romance

Girls' Camp: Lesbian Group Sex

Wet Dream: Ladyboy Fantasy Erotica

The Convent: Taboo Sex with a Nun

Sex Robot: A Dream Sex Machine

The Personal Trainer: Getting Pumped at the Gym

The Dominatrix: BDSM Lesbian Domination

Webcam Chat: Lesbian Online Sex

Paint Me: A Kinky Bodypainting Workshop

The Toy Party: Girls Sharing Sex Toys

The Costume Party: Strapping One On

Swedish Sauna: Lesbian Group Sex

The Therapist: Taboo Lesbian Erotica

Elevator Shaft: Bisexual Threesomes Erotica

Ladyboy: Lesbian Transgender Erotica

Peep Show: Lesbian Voyeur Erotica

The Dare: Public Sex Erotica

Maid Service: Lesbian Threesomes Erotica

The Hitchhiker: First Time Lesbian Erotica

The Housesitter: Spycam Lesbian Erotica

The Spa: Lesbian Group Orgy

Parlor Games: Blindfold Sex Party

The Exchange Student: First Time Lesbian Erotica

The Hostel: Bisexual Group Erotica

The Harem: Lesbian Erotic Romance

The Orient Express: Lesbian Voyeur Erotica

The First Lady: A Forbidden Lesbian Erotic Romance

The Slave: Lesbian BDSM Erotica

The Masseuse: Lesbian Sensuous Erotica

Too Close for Comfort: Lesbian Forbidden Erotica

Naked Twister: A Wild Party Game

Lexi: The Sex App (Lesbian Fantasy Erotica)

Call Girl: Lesbian Bisexual Threesomes Erotica

Circle Jill: Lesbian Masturbation Workshop

The Viewing Room: Masturbation Voyeur Erotica

Spin the Bottle: A Kinky Party Game

The Hair Salon: Lesbian Voyeur Erotica

Tribadism 1: Girls Only Sex Workshop

Tribadism 2: The Art of Scissoring

Tribadism 3: Threeway Hookups

The Kiss: A Game of Oral Sex

Pledge Week: Sorority Sisters

Carny Games 1: A Wild Sex Party

Carny Games 2: A Kinky Sex Party

Carny Games 3: An Erotic Sex Party

Dreamscape: An Artificial Reality Game

Glory Hole: Guess Who's On the Other Side

Joy Ride: A Late Night Erotic Bus Trip

The Blind Girl: An Erotic Romance(Coming Soon)

Lesbian Erotica Bundles:

Jade's Erotic Adventures: Books 1 - 5

Jade's Erotic Adventures: Books 6 - 10

Jade's Erotic Adventures: Books 11 - 15

Jade's Erotic Adventures: Books 16 - 20

Jade's Erotic Adventures: Books 21 - 25

Jade's Erotic Adventures: Books 26 - 30

Jade's Erotic Adventures: Books 31 - 35

Jade's Erotic Adventures: Books 36 - 40

Jade's Erotic Adventures: Books 41 - 45

Jade's Erotic Adventures: Books 46 - 50

Fifty Shades of Jade: Superbundle

Standalone Stories:

The Polynesian Girl: A Lesbian EroticRomance

For the uninhibited...

1

I first noticed her while walking downtown on a blustery summer day. A waif-like girl, not more than a hundred pounds, walking slowly through a busy intersection in downtown Chicago. Her long brown hair was blowing in the wind but it was the soft tapping of the pavement in front of her that attracted my attention. I peered down and noticed the rhythmic swinging of a white cane in front of her body. She seemed oblivious to the movement of the noisy traffic around her, holding her sunglass-clad head upright and steady as she strode confidently through the crossing. I didn't notice the blur of yellow while I glanced at her exquisite ass in her skinny jeans, clinging to her shapely figure like the tights of a ballerina. But when the taxi honked his horn angrily as he sped around the corner on a red light, I leapt instinctively ahead of her and slammed my palms loudly on the hood of his car.

"Watch where you're going, asshole!" I screamed, glaring at the driver through his windscreen while I blocked his progress with my legs straddling the front of his grille. "Are you *blind?* Can't you see people are crossing the lane?"

"Sorry," the cab driver shrugged, sticking her head outside his window. "The girl was walking so slowly, I was just trying to get ahead of the crowd."

"Not *everybody's* in a hurry, buddy," I said, shaking my head. "You should be more careful, you could have run someone over."

By now, the pretty blind girl and the rest of the passing pedestrians had traversed the intersection, pausing briefly on the other side to stare at me while they waited for the light to change at the adjacent crossing. When the signal turned green and the cars queued up behind the taxi began to honk their horns impatiently, I slapped my hands once again on the cab's hood and grudgingly moved out of his way.

"Thanks," the blind girl said when I joined her on the other side of the street. "But I had it under control. I heard him coming and was about to slow down."

"I didn't know," I said, peering down at her equally tight sweater, showcasing her perky breasts and hourglass figure. "You just looked so vulnerable walking alone like that through the busy intersection. I don't know why the city allows cars to turn right on a red, especially at the height of rush hour. Somebody's liable to get killed one of these days..."

"Not to worry," the girl chuckled. "It's not like I haven't done this before. I'm used to crazy cab drivers by now."

"You're not worried about not being able to *see* them?" I said.

"I can *hear* them approaching long before they pose any threat," the girl nodded. "I've developed a pretty sharp sense of awareness using my other senses. You'd be surprised what a blind person can do with only her hearing and a long enough cane."

"I'm sorry about that *blind* comment I made to the driver," I said, suddenly feeling self-conscious about my thoughtless interjection. "That was insensitive of me."

"No worries," the girl laughed. "It's just a figure of speech. I'm used to it by now."

"I suspect it's much more than that to you. Please accept my apologies."

"Why don't you let me buy you a coffee to thank you for your kindness?" the girl said, tapping her cane softly against the side of my shoe. "That is, if you're not in as much of a hurry as the impatient cab driver..."

"No–I mean *yes*," I stammered, flushing lightly at the girl's invitation.

"Great," she smiled, crooking her free arm. "There's a little shop around the corner that serves the best coffee in town. Why don't you let me show you the way?"

"Okay," I said, slipping my arm between hers and feeling my skin tingle as she stepped off the curb and began tapping her cane on the pavement while she pulled me closer to her.

I had to smile at the irony of a blind girl leading me through this part of the city, where I already knew the location of virtually every coffee shop and upscale clothing store next to the Miracle Mile, having lived here most of my life. But I was happy to find any excuse to get closer to her, feeling the soft brush of her fuzzy mohair sweater rubbing against my exposed skin. When we reached the entrance to the shop, she opened the door for me and I stepped tentatively inside, breathing in the heavenly scent of the exotic coffees brewing behind the counter.

"What will you have?" the girl asked, turning towards me as she approached the cashier.

"I feel like *indulging* today," I smiled, scanning the hand-drawn menu on the large chalkboard hanging over the far wall. "How about a caramel macchiato?"

"For the lady," the girl said, nodding toward the barista. "And I'll have an Americano."

There was an awkward silence while the barista turned to prepare our drinks, then the girl reached out to squeeze my arm.

"Why don't you find us a free table near the window?" she said. "I like to feel the sun on my face while I sip my coffee. I'll join you in a few minutes."

"Okay," I said, not used to being the submissive one, especially in the company of a supposedly handicapped partner.

I found a table in the corner of the shop and sat down, watching the girl effortlessly pay for the coffees while tapping her credit card over the point-of-sale terminal lying next to the cash register, then she picked up the drinks and walked in the direction of our table, slowing down just in time to place the steaming coffees deftly on the surface in front of me.

"Yours is the bigger cup," she said, sitting down opposite me while she angled her cane gently over her lap.

"Thanks," I said, picking up the cup and taking a quick sip of the tangy brew, humming approvingly at the sweet taste of the exotic concoction. "But how did you know where to find me?"

"I followed your scent," the girl smiled. "You're wearing a lovely perfume. Is that Yves Saint Laurent?"

"Yes, Black Opium," I said, widening my eyes at her surprising sense of perceptiveness. "How did you know?"

"I've got a keen sense of smell," the girl nodded. "I suppose it's somewhat overdeveloped because of my loss of sight."

The girl gently removed the lid of her cup and cradled it between her hands while lifting it slowly under her nose. She inhaled deeply and smiled with a slight upturn of her lips, then she tilted the mug between her parted lips, sucking back a small mouthful while she hummed softly, swirling the elixir inside her mouth before swallowing it like a gentle rivulet in a babbling stream. I'd never seen anyone drink their coffee so sensuously, and suddenly I felt self-conscious about wolfing down my overly flavored coffee so quickly.

"I'm Jade," I said, practically choking on my next mouthful as I studied the soft curves of her face. I couldn't see her eyes behind her dark glasses, but her countenance reminded me of a young Audrey Hepburn from the movie Breakfast at Tiffany's.

"Juliet," the girl nodded, raising her cup toward mine in a gesture of goodwill.

"Jade and Juliet," I smiled at the lyrical alliteration of our names. "Something tells me that near-miss with the taxi wasn't just by chance. I have a feeling we were meant to cross paths today."

"Maybe so," Juliet smiled with a soft flush of her face. Now it was *her* turn to betray the growing attraction between us...

2

———

Juliet and I chatted for an hour or so in the coffee shop, then we decided to go for a stroll along the waterfront park toward her home near the Navy Pier. We talked about our lives growing up in Chicago, and I learned that her blindness was caused by a congenital condition that caused her to lose her sight in early childhood. By the time we reached the end of the park, neither of us were ready to separate, and we hesitated awkwardly outside the entrance to her upscale condominium building.

"Is this where you live?" I said, peering up at the tall, gleaming tower overlooking the lake.

"Yes," Juliet said. "Would you like to come inside? There's a magnificent view from the forty-fourth floor. Or so I've been told."

"Um, sure," I said, suddenly feeling my panties dampening at the possibility of making love to this mysterious and alluring blind girl.

"I'd like to stop by the market first," she said. "I need to pick up some food for dinner. Will you join me? I make a mean mushroom risotto."

"Mmm, sounds delicious," I said. "You're twisting my arm."

"It's a date, then," Juliet said, grabbing my hand and pulling me in the direction of the Whole Foods store one block away.

When we entered the store, Juliet went to the produce section and I watched her, bemused, as she sampled and chose the ingredients for the meal. First, she picked up a large portobello mushroom from the display case and caressed it gently with her fingers, like she was squeezing a plump breast. After placing it in her cart, she selected a long zucchini and bent it softly in her hands, stroking and squeezing it like an oversize cock. When she raised a tuft of parsley and buried her nose in it, smelling its bouquet like it was a woman's sex, I practically came right there in the aisle. For the next twenty minutes, I followed her through the store, amazed at how easily she moved from aisle to aisle, shaking the boxes and feeling the shapes of the jars to select exactly what she needed. When we reached the liquor section, she turned to me and smiled.

"Would you like to choose the wine?" she said.

"For making the *risotto*, or as a side accompaniment?"

"Both. Something crisp and dry, like a pinot Grigio or Sauvignon blanc."

I scanned the bottle labels and chose a moderately priced pinot with a good rating then one of my favorite chardonnays for the pairing, and placed them in the cart.

"Done," I said, suddenly feeling my stomach rumbling at the thought of sitting down for the delicious meal.

"Good," she said. "Let's head to the check-out and blow this pop-stand. I'm starved!"

When we got to the check-out lane, I volunteered to pay for the groceries since she'd paid for the coffees earlier, but she insisted on covering the cost since she'd invited me, so I bagged the items while she paid at the terminal. When we returned to her building, we took the elevator to the top floor, and I gasped when she opened the door to her suite and I saw the expansive view of the lake through her floor-to-ceiling windows.

"Wow!" I exclaimed, admiring the clean esthetic of her beautifully appointed apartment. "This place is *gorgeous*. Do you live here all by yourself?"

"Most of the time," she nodded, leading me into her open-air kitchen and placing the bags on the counter. "Why don't you enjoy the view while I start preparing dinner? It should be ready in an hour or so."

I walked out onto the terrace and gazed out over the blue horizon which seemed to stretch out forever, and breathed in the fresh scent of the lake breeze wafting in from the East. The terrace was almost as big as my back yard, with beautiful wicker furniture and a gleaming Viking grill, and I wondered how a blind girl could afford to live independently like this. When I returned to the kitchen, I could already smell the savory scent of the rice and the broth cooking in the stovetop pan.

"Can I help with something?" I said.

"Why don't you chop the onions and zucchini while I keep an eye on the rice?" Juliet said.

As I chopped the vegetables, Juliet sliced the portobello mushrooms into thin wedges on a separate cutting board and minced the parsley using curled fingers to blunt the sharp edge of the knife. I continued to be amazed at how easily she was able to do everything sighted people took for granted, and while I had the chance, I soaked up her beautiful figure in her tight-fitting clothes, knowing I could ogle her with impunity. She'd finally taken her sunglasses off and

I studied her beautiful brown eyes staring straight ahead, not recognizing any sign of impairment.

"Everything okay over there?" she said, sensing my distraction. "You seem a little pensive..."

"I was just wondering how you can afford such a beautiful penthouse apartment. I never asked what you do for a living."

"*Nothing*, mostly," Juliet said. "My father's an investment banker and he seems to have a knack for picking the right stocks. I've never really wanted for anything as long as I can remember."

"You don't miss being able to *see*? I mean, since you weren't born blind. You once had the faculty, then lost it."

"It's been so long now, I can barely remember. But I do remember our frequent visits to the family cottage. I guess that's why I chose an apartment on the lakefront. I enjoy the smell of the water and the sound of the waves breaking over the shore."

"What do you do to keep busy?" I said, peering into the living room and noticing a baby grand piano sitting next to the large sectional sofa. "Does your family visit fairly often?"

"From time to time," Juliet nodded. "I dabble in a little songwriting and do yoga on the terrace between long walks downtown."

"That explains your perfect figure," I smiled, catching another quick peek of her tight ass. "You certainly seem self-sufficient in most ways."

"Not *every* way," she smiled. "It's nice to have some female company for a change."

"Oh?" I said, fishing for more details. "No boyfriends on the horizon?"

"Not since high school," Juliet laughed. "I find them a bit clumsy. Besides, they only seem interested in one thing..."

"I know what you mean," I said, feeling my pussy twitching when I learned she was single. "My first husband couldn't find his way around a woman's body if he had a magnifying glass. He might as well have been–"

"*Blind?*" Juliet said, pausing the stirring of the risotto in the pan.

"Sorry," I coughed. "I just meant it as another figure of speech. I'm going to have to be more careful around you."

"Please don't," Juliet said, stirring the broth more vigorously and tipping a sample up toward her lips. "I like your free spirit. It's refreshing to be with someone who doesn't treat me with kid gloves."

"I wouldn't *dream* of it," I said, scooping up some chunks of onion and zucchini from the cutting board and sprinkling them into the pan over her delicate fingers.

~

When the meal was finally ready, the two of us repaired to her small but elegant dining room, where we sat kitty-corner at the edge of the table overlooking the lake while we listened to soft jazz playing over the stereo. We made small talk for a while, feeling the increasing sexual tension between the two of us, then as we neared the end of the meal, Juliet stretched her right hand over the table toward my idle left hand and interlaced her fingers with mine, caressing my hand softly.

"Would you like something for dessert?" she said.

I peered into her eyes, angled down toward our joined hands.

"Yes," I said. "But not *food*. At least not the kind you were thinking. I've been dying to eat you up practically since the moment I met you."

"Good," she said, squeezing my hand more firmly. "Because unlike you, I haven't had a chance to examine your body properly, and I've been looking forward to squeezing something other than mushrooms and zucchini for a change..."

3

———

Juliet led me into her bedroom and lit some soft candles, then the two of us danced to the music playing in the other room as we slowly undressed one another. When we were fully disrobed, we fell onto the bed, twisting our bodies together while we moaned in each other's mouths. Now that I'd finally seen her body naked for the first time, I was even more turned on by her perfect ballerina figure, squeezing her small but firm breasts while sliding my fingers down the crack of her perfectly round ass. But Juliet wasn't about to let me have all the fun, and she quickly flipped me onto my back while sitting upright overtop of my hips.

"It's my turn to explore *your* body now," she smiled. "You didn't think I knew you were staring at my butt the whole time I was stirring the risotto?"

"I had to do *something* to keep myself distracted from the growing wet spot in my pants," I purred, staring up at her luminous face. "You've kept me waiting so long, I had to satisfy myself by making love to you with my eyes."

"Well, I suppose I'll have to settle for studying you with

my *fingers* now that I've got you exactly where I want you," she said, sliding the tips of her fingers gently over the top of my forehead and across my eyelids while she hummed softly.

She rolled her thumbs over the crest of my brow, nodding approvingly.

"You have beautiful *eyebrows*," she said. "Full, and perfectly trimmed, with a lovely arch..."

"You can tell all of this just from using your *fingers*?" I said, flaring my eyes open.

"You'd be surprised by the things I can discern using my fingers," she grinned, continuing her gentle exploration of my face.

"I can imagine," I panted, feeling my pussy beginning to dampen again. "You practically had me coming just watching you feel the vegetables at the food market."

"I might have been channeling something else while I was sampling the produce. You weren't the *only* one with lascivious thoughts on your mind."

"Mmm," I moaned, rolling my hips impatiently while she slid her fingers over my cheekbones and around the outline of my lips. "I can't wait for you to slide those fingers a little lower on my body..."

"In due course," she said. "Most of the fun is in the build-up."

"Maybe," I nodded. "It gives me all the more time to stare at your beautiful tits."

"You don't think they're too *small*?" she said.

"Are you kidding me?" I said, reaching out to circle her hard nipples with my fingertips. "They're absolutely perfect. If you weren't pinning me to the mattress, I'd be sucking them into my mouth right now."

"All in due time," Juliet smiled, using her elbows to push

my arms away from her body while she continued to caress me. "Lie still while I finish examining you."

"It's not going to be so easy if you keep touching me like that."

"Would you rather I sit on your *face* to keep you still?"

"In due course," I teased. "I'm way ahead of you..."

"Mmm," Juliet purred, sliding her fingers over the fullness of my lips while pressing her thumbs inside my moist cavity. "I'm looking forward to feeling these pretty lips sucking my *pearl*. They're very full and moist."

"Those aren't the *only* lips that are full and moist right now," I grunted, biting the knuckle of her thumb while I circled the tip of my tongue over her digit.

"So I can see," Juliet said, rolling her dripping pussy over my slippery mound while she stared straight ahead toward the headboard.

It was strange not being able to look into her eyes while she sat on top of me and explored my body, but there was something erotic about watching her meditative gaze as she had her way with me. It was as if she was channeling all of her senses through her fingertips while she caressed every crevasse and curve of my body. And she wasn't the only one whose other senses were over-stimulated from the suppression of another. I closed my eyes and savored every stroke of her fingers, feeling the pores of my skin tingling with goose bumps while our commingled juices dribbled down the front of my pussy.

"And this jaw..." she said, sliding her hands along the side of my face and fingering the crease of my chin with both thumbs. "So strong, yet feminine. And perfectly symmetrical, just like the rest of your face. You must have a long line suitors, looking as pretty as this."

"Not as many as you might imagine," I frowned, peering

up at her. "I seem to be the one always making the first move–"

"Like when you leapt in front of me to save me from the errant cab driver earlier today?" she smiled.

"I didn't do that to make a *pass* at you, at least not at first," I laughed. "Although I *was* mesmerized by your exquisite ass before I saw him swinging in front of you."

"Mm-hmm," Juliet huffed unconvinced, circling her fingers around my throat. "You sighted people have an unfair advantage."

"I'm not so sure about that," I grunted, feeling the electricity between us ramping up as she pinned me to the bed. "I'm starting to think your lack of sight has given you some kind of superpowers. I've never felt so turned on from a woman's touch before."

"Oh?" Juliet smiled, loosening her grip around my neck. "Is this your first time being with a woman this way?"

"No, but it's the first time I've almost come watching her touch something other than my *pussy*."

"You know," she grinned, tickling her fingers down the front of my chest toward my tingling breasts. "Some women can climax just *imagining* erotic thoughts. I've done so more than once listening to some of my favorite audiobooks."

"Without *touching* yourself?" I said, tilting my head up. "Who are your favorite authors?"

"I've got quite a few, but one of my favorites is Anais Nin. I love the way she can arouse my desire with her flowery prose, never resorting to crude words."

"That's ironic," I said, reflecting back on the time when my best friend Hannah tested my mettle by stimulating me remotely while I read one of Anais' books publicly in a crowded cafe. "I've had an orgasm reading one of her books too, although I confess it was under slightly different circumstances–"

"That sounds kind of *kinky*," Juliet said, circling her middle fingers around my swelling nipples while I felt her soft breath breathing down over my belly. "Do tell."

"Perhaps another time," I said, not wanting to interrupt her flow. "I'm enjoying a *different* kind of stimulation right now."

"Your nipples are quite large," she said, fingering my protruding bullets. "And *hard*. I'm looking forward to *fucking* them a little later after I'm finished exploring your body."

"Such naughty words," I teased. "I thought you didn't like using those."

"I didn't say *I* didn't," she smiled. "I just like it when others can arouse me in different ways sometimes. But I like it rough and dirty, too."

"Mmm," I moaned, rolling my hips more vigorously as my pussy twitched and dribbled down the middle of my slit. "I'm imagining you soiling my nipples with your pretty pussy right now..."

"Do you think it's pretty?" Juliet said, rocking her hips in synchronicity with mine while she pinched my nipples. "I noticed that yours is shaved, while mine is all hairy and unkempt."

"Sometimes messy is good," I rasped, arching my back as she pinched my nipples harder. "It's rare to find a woman with a natural bush these days."

"It sounds like you've been naked with a *lot* of women in your time," Juliet said, tightening her grip on my nipples.

"Perhaps a few," I grunted from the mixture of pleasure and pain she was giving me. "But none as mysterious and beautiful as you."

"You probably say that to all of your lovers," Juliet huffed

"Well, I've never been with a *blind* woman before," I said, reaching up to caress her small tits. "Nor one with such a perfect ass or breasts..."

"I haven't found any imperfections in *you* either," she said, squeezing my breasts before slipping her knee between my legs and sliding her dripping pussy over the top of my right thigh.

"You haven't even gotten halfway finished yet," I chuckled. "I'm sure you'll find a few things askew once you get a little lower."

"I can't *imagine*," she said, sliding the tips of her fingers down the indentation in the center of my abdomen and stopping as she pressed her thumb slowly into my navel. "Even your *bellybutton* is perfect, with its tiny little hole and tight hood."

"Oh my God," I groaned, humping my pussy over the front of her knee. "I see what you mean about coming without direct genital contact. If you keep stimulating me like this, I"m going to climax long before you get anywhere near my pussy."

"We'll have to see about that," she said, sliding further down my leg and grinding her wet labia over the top of my knee. "But not if you keep *cheating* like that."

"You're killing me!" I protested as she tickled the rim of my navel with the tip of her finger.

"I hope so," she smiled. "Did you know the French call an orgasm *petite mort*, meaning little death? I'm planning to kill you one caress at a time."

4

"The closer your fingers get to my nether regions, the more you're getting there," I said, spreading my now unconfined legs further apart for her to see the rivers of lubrication running down my slit and between the crack of my ass, leaving a large wet spot on her bed.

"So I can see," she said, sliding her hand over the sheets in front of my pussy while she caressed my shaved mound with her other hand. "I like your smooth mound. I can't even feel any stubble."

"I had it lasered a while ago," I nodded. "It was too much trouble keeping it shaved with a sharp razor blade."

"I can imagine," Juliet said, sliding her thumbs over the crest of my mound, millimeters from the edge of my throbbing clit. "Even more so for a *blind* girl."

"I'll be happy to do the honors if you feel like giving it a try sometime," I said. "It's a singular pleasure licking a woman's pussy when it's bare and exposed in all its glory."

"We'll have to see about that," Juliet said. "I'd like to sample yours first before taking the leap."

"Yes, please," I said, raising my aching pussy higher off the bed, closer to her face.

"Soon enough," Juliet teased. "I'm not finished cataloguing your body. I want to know every curve and cranny before I take you to paradise."

"Two can play that game," I said with a sly grin. "Just wait until it's my turn to stimulate *you*. I'm going to make you squeal and squirm just as much as you did to me before I kill you with pleasure."

"I hope so," Juliet said, pressing the tips of her fingers over the bony prominence of my pelvis before sliding them sensuously over the tops of my trembling thighs.

"I see that you haven't shaved *these*, at least," she said, levitating her hands barely above the surface of my skin, feeling the soft hairs of my thighs standing on end as she teased and tormented me.

"Not my *upper* legs," I groaned. "Thankfully, those hairs don't grow as long and thick as the ones on my shins."

"Mmm," Juliet nodded, sliding her palms over my knees and across the curvature of my inner calves. "Your legs have a beautiful tone and shape to them. Slender but firm, like a dancer's. I can tell you take care of yourself."

"I go to the gym and do a little yoga," I nodded, contracting my calves unconsciously as she squeezed and caressed them. "It gets harder the older you get. I think I've got a few extra years on you."

"Oh?" Juliet said, stopping the movement of her hands temporarily. "I never would have guessed from the firmness and suppleness of your skin. Exactly how much older are you, exactly?"

"I'm thirty-six. And I'm guessing you're closer to–"

"Twenty-two," Juliet said.

"Does our age difference give you pause?" I said, worried

that the halting of her caresses foreshadowed something more serious.

"Not in the least," she said, continuing to run her palms down the lower part of one leg and over the curve of my anklebone. "Unlike some *sighted* people, I don't have the handicap of biasing my impressions on the age and beauty of my partners."

"I never thought of it that way," I said, feeling a stronger attachment to this exotic beauty the longer we spent together. "I suppose there are certain advantages to missing some perceptions, after all."

"There are pluses and minuses," she nodded, slipping her hand around the base of my heel and softly caressing the sole of my foot while massaging the top surface with her other hand. "I've just found a way to maximize the advantages."

"You certainly have," I nodded, closing my eyes while I savored her sensuous foot massage. "If you're ever need a *job*, you'd make one hell of a professional masseuse."

"The kind in a *massage parlor*, or the therapeutic kind?"

"You seem to be exquisitely skilled at both," I purred.

"But the erotic kind might be more *fun*," she smiled.

"Certainly for the *recipient*," I said, rolling my hips suggestively, signaling for her to begin moving her hands back up higher on my tingling body.

"Are you growing impatient for a happy ending?" she said, spreading my feet wider apart and squatting her knees between my parted legs.

"I'm enjoying the journey," I said. "I'm just not sure about your final destination."

"Neither am I," Juliet grinned, squeezing my ankles tightly and sliding her palms slowly up the inside of my lower legs. "Sometimes it's fun just following the road to see where it takes you."

"Well, if you continue following *that* route, I assure you that the junction of those two roads will lead you to a rewarding place."

"Rewarding for you, or rewarding for me?"

"I suppose that depends on what you do when you get there," I grinned. "I didn't ask if you'd been with a woman this way before, also. There are so many ways two women can please each other by rubbing certain parts of their bodies together–"

"You mean like *this*?" Juliet said, sliding her thumbs over my knees and turning her palms inward as she inched closer to my quivering pussy.

"Among other ways," I panted, feeling my juices running down my slit like a waterfall.

"How about like *this*?" she said, leaning her body forward and blowing softly on my dripping petals.

"Fuck, yes," I groaned.

"Mmm, I like it when you talk dirty," Juliet purred.

"Suck my pussy, Juliet," I huffed. "I want to feel your pretty rosebud lips over my hot clit."

"Mmm," Juliet purred. "I can feel the heat from your opening. But I want to tease you for just a little longer..."

"You're driving me *crazy*," I protested, thrashing my hips wildly in front of her lips. "How much longer are you going to make me wait? I want to come all over your face so badly..."

"That depends on you," Juliet smiled, blowing harder on my erect gland while squeezing the bottom of my upper thighs under my wet ass with her thumbs, inches away from my swollen folds. "You just have to use your imagination a little harder."

"I'm already dreaming of all the ways I want to make love to you," I grunted. "I'm going to come so hard the moment you touch me."

"I'm *already* touching you," Juliet grinned.

"I mean on my sensitive spot. I'm going to explode any moment now..."

"Yes, baby," Juliet purred as she brought her face closer to my quivering pussy while she squeezed my shaking thighs more firmly. "Close your eyes and lose yourself in the feeling. I can feel you getting closer..."

"Oh God, oh God," I huffed, feeling my orgasm coming on like a freight train the more she blew on my engorged clit. "I'm going to come, Juliet. I'm going to come so hard. Oh *fuckkkkk!"*

I probably should have warned Juliet about my tendency to squirt when I had powerful orgasms, but I'd been so lost in the buildup that I completely lost sight of everything else beyond my growing pleasure. When my orgasm finally washed over me, I felt my contractions clamping down inside my pussy as my pelvic floor muscles began pulsing, ejecting huge spurts of ejaculatory fluid and vaginal juices all over her surprised face. But bless her heart, for she didn't flinch while I ejected one long, hard spray after another over her pretty face while I jerked and screamed at the top of my lungs. It took well over a minute for me to finish convulsing and squirting, and when I finally relaxed my clenched butt muscles and collapsed my body back down onto the soaking bed, I flared my eyes open, shocked at how easily the blind girl had brought me to a powerful orgasm simply by caressing every part of my body beyond the obvious places, using only her fingers and the power of suggestion.

"There now," she said, sliding her body next to mine and kissing me softly. "That wasn't so bad after all, was it?"

"Are you kidding me?" I panted, still coming down from my intense climax. "I don't think I've *ever* come that hard. And you did it by barely touching me."

"Well, I was touching you," Juliet said. "Just not in the usual places."

"It's true, what you said earlier," I said, feeling her soft breasts pressing against mine. "Sometimes you only need to use your imagination to enjoy the most sublime of experiences."

"Yes," Juliet said, grinding her mound softly against mine. "Although there's something to be said for taking a more *direct* approach from time to time."

"I know what you mean," I said, this time rolling her over onto *her* back and pinning her to the mattress. "And this time, I have no intention of treating you with kid gloves..."

5

____

I sat up on top of Juliet's hips the way she'd done with me earlier and swiped my still-dripping pussy over her soft bush. As she rolled her hips in tandem with me, moaning softly, I peered down into her vacant eyes staring straight ahead, feeling guilty about using her for my own pleasure.

"What's it like?" I said, pausing our movement. "I mean, making love to somebody without being able to see them?"

"Much the same as I imagine it is for sighted people," Juliet said. "The feelings are the same, and just as pleasurable. Maybe even *more* so, because we're focused even more on our sense of touch."

"I suppose that makes sense," I nodded. "I'm beginning to feel a bit handicapped myself, distracted as I am by your pretty face and beautiful figure while I touch you..."

"Why don't you try it for yourself, *without* your sense of sight?" Juliet said. "I have a silk scarf in my armoire that you could use as a blindfold."

"That *does* sound intriguing," I said, feeling my pussy twitching involuntarily. "But I'm worried I might poke you in the face with an errant elbow or knee, not having your innate sense of space and movement."

"You get used to it faster than you might imagine," Juliet laughed. "You already know where the important parts are. Haven't you ever made love in the dark before?"

"Of course," I said. "Let's give it a shot. At the very least, it'll be a fun experiment and give me a chance to put myself in your shoes."

"Absolutely," Juliet smiled. "Besides, *I've* never made love to a blind girl either."

"Save that thought," I said, rolling off her hips and jumping off the bed. "I'll be back in a flash."

It didn't take long to find her Hermes scarf hanging next to her camel-hair dress coat, and I folded it over three times to make sure the fabric was completely opaque before tying it tightly around the back of my head and pulling the edges over the bottom of my eyes to block out all of my peripheral vision.

"This is a bit *scary*," I said, holding out my arms in front of me and taking some slow steps back in the direction of her bed. "I'm not familiar with the arrangement of your furniture and I'm operating in the dark for the first time."

"Just go slow and follow my voice–" Juliet purred from the bed.

I slammed my knee against her sideboard and cursed softly under my breath.

"Shit!" I groaned. "It looks like it's going to take me a little longer to acclimate to your surroundings than you have."

"Here," Juliet said, reaching out her hand. "Feel my hand and let me guide you the rest of the way."

I reached my right hand out awkwardly in front of me and swiped it from side to side until I felt her hand, then she clasped my fingers softly with mine, pulling me onto the bed beside her. We kissed for a few minutes and I purred into her mouth, focusing on the feeling of her soft lips and the fresh taste of her saliva.

"Mmm," I mewed. "Somehow this feels different than kissing someone with my eyes closed..."

"*Good* different or *bad* different?" Juliet said.

"Good, I think," I nodded, running my fingers through her hair as we probed each other's mouths with our tongues. "It's forcing me to focus on my other sensations."

"Are you finding those sensations *pleasurable*?"

"Your hair feels incredibly soft and silky," I nodded. "And your lips feel even fuller than I remembered from before."

"Well, they might be a little more puffed up than usual from the stimulation of your tongue right now," she said.

"Good," I smiled. "Hopefully some *other* parts of you are also getting puffed up from my stimulation."

"I don't think you have to worry about that," Juliet said, pressing her moistening pussy against my thigh as I pushed my knee between her legs.

"I want to taste and feel every part of your body like this," I said, kissing my way slowly down her neck while I felt the twitch of her muscles and the drops of her sweat as her body involuntarily responded to my touch.

"I never answered your question earlier," she said.

"Which question is that?" I said.

"The one about whether I'd been with another woman like this before. And the answer is no, unless you count some playful teasing under the covers during elementary school sleepovers."

"Well you certainly seem to know your way around a woman's body, for someone who's never had sex with one before."

"That hasn't stopped me from fantasizing about it, or learning from all the sexy audiobooks I've listened to."

"Well, you certainly seem to be a quick learner," I chuckled.

"As are you," she said, arching her back and groaning softly as my tongue reached her firm mounds and I began circling her hardening berries with my tongue.

"I love your small tits," I murmured. "They're so soft and firm. But not as hard as your *nipples*. I can feel the skin around them puckering..."

"My whole *body* is puckering," Juliet groaned. "I can feel my hairs standing on end, and the hood of my clit retracting."

"Oh my *God*," I panted. "Are you trying to make me come again before I touch you down there? Because my imagination is running wild right now..."

"I hope not," Juliet smiled. "I need all of your attention focused on me right now or I'm liable to explode before you get to the interesting places."

"These places are plenty interesting enough," I mumbled, alternately sucking each of her nipples until I was satisfied they were as hard and swollen as I could make them. "I'll be coming back to give them some more attention soon enough."

"Mmm," Juliet moaned, rolling her body sensuously on the bed while I stimulated her with my tongue. "I love the sensation of your lips licking my body," she said. "*Every* part of my body."

"I'm glad," I smiled. "But you still haven't experienced my most *talented* skill. I have a fair amount of experience licking women in a few *other* private places..."

"God, yes," Juliet grunted, rolling her hips aggressively, begging me to go lower on her body.

"All in due course, my love," I grinned.

"You're such a *tease*," Juliet huffed, crossing her arms over her chest in feigned anger while I tickled my way down the middle of her stomach with the tip of my tongue.

"I learned from the best," I smiled, playfully kissing her as I rimmed the outside of her navel with my tongue.

"That feels so good," she rasped, rocking her hips more vigorously.

"Are you channeling me licking you somewhere *else*?" I said.

"Let's just say that my imagination is running way ahead of you..."

"Don't come *too* fast," I grinned. "I want to feel your bean twitching in my mouth when you climax."

"It won't take long at *this* rate, I assure you."

"I better slow down then," I teased. "I wouldn't want to ruin the mood. Besides, I'm enjoying tormenting you as much as you did me earlier."

"Next time, I won't make you wait as long," she said, tilting her head up to gaze in my direction. "I promise to touch you more directly. I'm *dying* to taste your sex."

"Famous last words," I chuckled. "I bet you say that to all your lovers."

"I *wish*," Juliet huffed, lifting her hips to meet my face as I lowered my head over her soft and fragrant bush.

"Your muff is even softer than my fur hat. And far better smelling."

"I'm not sure if that's *my* scent you're sensing or your own," Juliet said. "Your pussy was still pretty wet when you sat over my hips before putting on the blindfold."

"Maybe so," I said. "But I like the scent of our perfumes *commingling*. I plan on doing a lot more commingling with you before the night is over."

"I hope so," Juliet said, licking her lips expectantly. "I've read enough of Anais Nin's stories to know the many ways two women can satisfy one another."

"You have *no* idea," I smiled, sticking my nose in her muff and inhaling her scent like she'd done with the parsley at the market, before lowering my face further between her legs.

6

———————

When I felt how wet and slippery the insides of her thighs were, I turned my head and licked up her juices like the icing on the inside of a cake bowl, nibbling and teasing her around the perimeter of her steaming crotch. When she tried to push her body further down the bed to press her pussy into my mouth, I pulled away a few extra inches, blowing softly on her clit.

"Uhnnn," she groaned, swiping her arms down onto the mattress beside her and gripping the sheets tightly with two hands. "You're driving me crazy."

"How do you like it?" I taunted. "It's nice to be on the other end of this for a change."

"I like it," she panted. "But I'd like it a lot *more* if you'd tickle my button with those pretty, full lips of yours."

"I dunno," I smiled. "Maybe I'll just keep teasing you to see if you can climax from your imagination alone. I'm beginning to feel a little inadequate compared to your favorite author..."

"Oh no," Juliet protested. "I assure you, this feels way better than *listening* to someone describing the act. I just need to *see* what it actually feels like. I mean, to have another woman actually sucking my pussy."

"You poor thing," I said. "I'll acquiesce this time because it's your first time. I want to feel you climaxing just as much as you do."

"Yes, Jade," Juliet pleaded. "Suck me into your mouth. Show me what it feels like to make love to a woman. I've dreamed of this moment for so long–"

"Mmm," I hummed, lowering my face to her dripping pussy and licking up the middle of her dripping crease like it was a melting ice cream cone, then pausing when I reached the apex of her folds to wrap my lips around her flaring jewel and savor the sensation of her burning organ.

"Oh God," she grunted, pressing her pussy harder into my face. "That feels *so* much better than I imagined. Suck my clit, Jade. Lick me like you've licked all your other female partners."

"No way," I said, pulling my face away from her throbbing gland for a moment. "You're not like any of my other partners, and this is way different than all those other times."

"Because you're wearing a *blindfold* this time?"

"Partly," I said. "But you're different from all those other women. And not only because you're blind. You have a certain sweet innocence about you that I find especially arousing."

"Well, I'm glad you're the one I bumped into on the street to lose my innocence to. I can't imagine a more loving and tender partner for my first time."

"Oh Juliet," I said, feeling my heart pounding in my chest as my eyes watered under the blindfold while I circled her clit with my lips and felt myself growing closer to this mysterious and sexy blind girl. I rolled my tongue softly over her bulb and as she began to rock her hips in growing ecstasy, I circled the tip over her nub in figure-eight motions, caressing every part of her throbbing gland.

"Yes, Jade," Juliet huffed. "Don't stop. I'm going to come on your face any moment now..."

When I heard that she was moments away from climaxing, I pulled my face away from her burning pussy, feeling her legs twitching next to my cheeks.

"What are you doing?" Juliet protested. "I was just about to come!"

"I'm enjoying this way too much to let you come this fast," I said, listening to her pussy making wet slurping sounds as her vulva spasmed in a mini pre-climax. "Besides, I still haven't paid you back sufficiently for tormenting me earlier when I was prostrated in front of *you*."

"I promise I'll never do that again," Juliet pleaded, gyrating her hips rapidly in front of my blindfold-covered face. "I promise I'll suck your clit as hard and fast as you want whenever you ask me–"

"Is that the *only* way you're going to touch me?" I teased, blowing my cool breath over her puckering vulva.

"God no," Juliet hissed. "I'm going to fuck you with my cunt and my fingers and my toes and every other part of my body that can possibly make you squirm and squeal with. I'm going to do all the things my favorite author described and plenty more. That's all I could think about while I was preparing dinner."

"Good," I said. "Because I'm far from finished with you. This is just the appetizer before the main course."

I buried my face back in her steaming snatch and clenched my hands around her tightening buttocks, sucking her clit hard into my mouth while flapping my tongue faster over her glans, listening to the whimpers emanating from higher up on the bed as she inched closer to nirvana. While she slowly elevated her hips higher off the surface of the bed, my head followed her movement in lock-step, flicking her clit ever harder while tasting the juices running down the front of my chin.

When she finally climaxed with a loud animal grunt, jerking her pussy hard against my dripping face, I held her tightly in my arms, savoring every twitch and spasm of her exploding pussy. She didn't squirt like I had, but the combination of sensations I felt while holding her shaking body eclipsed anything I'd ever experienced before. I wasn't sure if it was because I was quickly falling in love with the pretty blind girl, or if it was because I was blindfolded when she came for the first time. Either way, it was the most erotic sensation I'd felt in a long time, and I didn't want to let go of her even after she stopped shaking against my face.

Besides, I smiled to myself. There'd be plenty of time to teach her how to gush and squirt when she climaxed. That was *one* special talent I'd be holding in reserve for the right moment.

7

Juliet and I made love three more times that night, then we fell asleep in each other's arms, resting peacefully until the light from the morning sun woke us up. I got out of bed and went to the kitchen to make coffee, and when I heard Juliet stirring, I brought her a steaming cup and placed it on her night table.

"Mmm," she purred, smelling the hot java. "That's a pleasant sensation to wake up to. I haven't had someone bring me coffee in bed since, well, *forever*."

"If you feel like staying in bed, I'd be happy to whip up some omelettes while we watch the sunrise together..."

"That sounds yummy," Juliet nodded. "I worked up quite an appetite from all those calories we burned last night."

"That wasn't the *only* thing burning," I smiled. "I haven't had sex that hot in a long time."

"Me neither," Juliet said, taking a sip of her coffee. "Except in my case, it's been like, *never*."

"Why don't you relax while I get breakfast, then maybe we can generate some more heat before we decide what to do for the rest of the day."

"You mean you're not sick of me yet?" she said, propping her head up on a bent elbow. "I thought maybe the novelty of making love to a blind girl might have worn off by now–"

"Hardly," I said, sitting down beside her on the bed and kissing her softly on her lips. "We're just getting started here. Besides, I like you for a lot more than just the sex. You're starting to grow on me."

"I like the sound of that," Juliet purred. "You better get out of here and start preparing breakfast or we're likely to never to get out of bed today."

"Save that thought," I smiled. "I'll be back in a flash..."

While I started making breakfast, I heard Juliet get out of bed and go to the washroom then she joined me in the kitchen wearing only a long sweater, wrapping her arms around my waist while I whipped the eggs in a bowl.

"Can I help with anything?" she said, kissing me softly on the back of my neck.

"Yes," I said, taking a peek at the bottom of her bare ass poking out of her sweater. "You can find something else to do so as to not distract me from my task. If you keep prancing around in that skimpy outfit, I'm likely to *burn* something."

"Okay," she said, turning around and shimmying her ass at me while she headed toward the living room. "Maybe just for a few minutes."

She walked toward the piano and sat down on the bench in front of it, beginning to play some soft music while I chopped the vegetables on the cutting board to the beat of her melody.

When astronauts go up in space, she started singing softly.
And look down at us
They don't see lines
Separating us...

I turned around and watched her sing while she turned her face up to the rising sun in the east. Her voice sounded like an angel, soft and delicate like a young Sarah McLaughlin. I couldn't place the melody or the lyrics, and I suddenly realized that she was singing a song she'd composed herself.

They see a jewel
Floating in the void of space
That we are privileged
To call our place...

I found myself swaying my body to her beautiful voice and the rhythmic melody, smiling at the timely subject of her composition.

But our blue planet
Where once man roamed with room to spare
Is now a place
Where people fight over who goes where...

Suddenly, her fingers began moving quicker over the keyboard as she developed a crescendo into the chorus.

If we all want to live in peace and unison
They we must believe from the moment of birth
That we are citizens of planet earth
'Cause we are one...

"Oh my God," I said, temporarily stopping my cooking and walking over to her position at the piano, resting my hand on the polished Steinway. "Did you *write* that song?"

"It's something I whipped up one day after listening to the news and hearing about another war," she nodded. "Do you like it?"

"Like it?" I said. "It's absolutely beautiful. Besides the

powerful message of the lyrics, the melody is uplifting and your voice is magnificent."

"Stop," Juliet said. "You're making me blush."

"I'm not kidding," I said. "Have you approached any agents or sent your material to any of the major record labels? This song could totally be a hit."

"I've never thought about writing my songs with the intention of going commercial–"

"Why don't you put it out on the internet then? I bet it would go viral in an instant. The record labels would be breaking down the doors to sign you. You could be the next Adele..."

"No thanks," Juliet said. "I'm happy leading my quiet life up here in the clouds. All that fame and attention isn't for me."

"Suit yourself," I said, furrowing my brows disappointingly. "I'm going to finish preparing breakfast while you serenade me. At least you've got *one* giant fan so far."

While I finished preparing the omelettes, I listened to Juliet singing some more songs, swaying my body rhythmically to the melody and her sweet voice, feeling my heart pounding and my eyes watering as she moved me to tears. By the time the meal was ready, I hated the idea of stopping her performance.

"I hate to interrupt your lovely concert," I said, placing the plates of food on her dining table. "I could stay here all day and listen to you playing. You're really tugging at my heartstrings."

"I'm glad," Juliet said, swiping the back of her hand softly over my cheekbones and feeling the trail of a tear rolling down the front of my face. "Is it just the *music* that's moving you this strongly?"

"No," I said, squeezing her hand more firmly. "I'm really starting to *fall* for you..."

"That makes two of us," Juliet said, smiling at me gently. "I have a feeling my *next* song will be about you."

8

A fter we finished breakfast, we talked about what we wanted to do for the rest of the day, and Juliet suggested going to the county fair.

"The county *fair*?" I said, widening my eyes. "Won't you get *vertigo* going on those rides? Plus, I'll have an unfair advantage playing all the games..."

"I wouldn't be so sure about that," Juliet winked. "Most of those games are rigged, anyway. They're more a matter of *luck* than skill. I used to go all the time when I was a kid. It's a huge thrill feeling my body being tossed around on the rides, not knowing where they're going to take me–"

"Ok," I said. "As long as you don't *throw up* on me. But I need to take a shower first before we head out. I don't want everyone smelling the scent of sex all over my body from last night."

"They'd barely notice over the aroma of popcorn, candy floss, and grilled hot dogs," Juliet laughed. "Do you mind if I join you? It might be kind of fun having a shower together."

"You're reading my mind, girl," I smiled, caressing her fingers as I wolfed down the last of my omelette. "We can clean this up afterwards. I've been dying to feel your lissome figure again, pretty much from the moment we woke up."

"Come, then," Juliet said, rising from the table and grasping my hand as she led me in the direction of her ensuite bathroom.

Her shower was bigger than I expected, with a large glass enclosure, dual shower heads, and a row of water jets lining the sides of the marble walls. After we stripped off our clothes and stepped inside, she twisted the taps and set the temperature to a steamy boil, then we stepped into the center of the spray, feeling the jets stimulating our skin while we melded our bodies together.

"Oh my God," I purred, slipping my tongue into her mouth. "This feels *heavenly*..."

"It feels even *more* heavenly if you position your hips in the right place," she smiled. "The water jets can be quite stimulating if you angle them a certain way."

She turned her body around to face one of the jets, then she tilted her hips upward until the spray squirted against her mound while she moaned softly. When I saw how she was stimulating herself, I pressed my tits against her wet back and humped her ass with my dripping pussy, feeling the spray jetting through our joined legs.

"Uhnnn," I grunted when I felt the powerful pulses between our slits. "Just when I thought this couldn't get any better. What *other* surprises have you got in store for me?"

"You'll have to wait until we get to the fair," she smiled, blinking her eyes under the overhead waterfall spray that was bouncing over our shoulders. "I play a pretty mean game of ring toss."

"I could probably snare one or two over your *nipples* right now," I said, rolling my hands over her slippery breasts and pinching her hardening teats. "That would be even more fun."

"Maybe," Juliet groaned, rocking her hips in synchronicity with me. "But I'm having plenty of fun playing *this* game right now."

"Do you want me to *soap you up*?" I said. "It might be more fun if we use our *hands* to enjoy this ride."

"Yes, please," Juliet mewed, angling her head over my shoulder to kiss my lips as the water cascaded over our faces.

I saw a bar of scented soap lying in the chrome rack on the side wall and picked it up, sliding it slowly under Juliet's arms and over her firm breasts.

"Mmm," she purred. "I love the way you touch me."

"And I love the way you *respond* to my touch," I said, feeling her tummy trembling while I swiped the bar lower and began lathering her hairy bush.

"I need to feel your fingers on my pussy again," Juliet grunted. "The combination of the warm spray, the slippery soap, and your soft hands is driving me crazy."

"Yes, baby," I hummed, echoing the lyrics to her song. "Surrender to the pleasure. 'Cause we are one..."

"You have a beautiful voice," Juliet moaned as I began fingering her clit. "Sing to me while you feel my body."

I paused for a moment while I thought about what I should sing to reflect our growing attraction, then I began warbling the Donny Hathaway song *A Song for You* in her ear.

I've been so many places in my life and time
I've sung a lot of songs, I've made some bad rhymes
I've acted out my life in stages
With ten thousand people watching
But we're alone now

And I'm singing this song to you...

"That's one of my favorite songs," she crooned, circling her hips faster while I jilled her clit harder. "I used to like the Michael Bublé version, but now I've got a new favorite cover artist."

"That's just because I'm playing with your pussy while I sing to you," I chuckled, sticking my little fingers into her dripping slit while I continued rubbing the slippery soap bar against her throbbing bean.

"Maybe," she shuddered. "But I could listen to you sing to me this way all day."

"Well, we can't stay inside *all* day," I grinned, dropping the bar of soap onto the shower floor while I circled her glans with my two forefingers and massaged her mound with my thumb. "We've got a date at the *fair*, remember?"

"Oh yeah," she grunted, tilting her hips further upward as she clenched her buttock muscles, edging closer to a climax. "Ring my bell, Jade. I'm ready to claim my prize."

"Uhnnn," I groaned along with her, feeling the powerful jet of water gushing between our joined hips while I circled her clit faster. "I'm going to come with you."

"*Fuck* yes," Juliet whimpered, her upper body becoming slack as her knees weakened near the height of ecstasy. "I'm coming, baby. Oh God, I'm coming for you. I love you so much..."

When she told me she loved me, it was like she'd flipped on another switch, and suddenly my pussy started convulsing in unison with hers while we both shook our bodies together under the undulating spray. When we finally came down from our highs, I held Juliet softly in my arms, savoring the feeling of the stimulating spray bathing us with its warmth.

"I love you too, Juliet," I whispered into her ear. "You've

opened my eyes to a whole new world of joy and tenderness."

"You've opened *mine,* too," Juliet said, turning her body around and pressing our bodies together while we kissed passionately under the steaming shower spray.

9

After Juliet and I got cleaned up, we took the train out to my place in the suburbs, then we drove my car to Lake County, where the annual fair was being held. When we entered the fairgrounds, we bought some candy floss, plastering the sticky strings of pastel candy all over our faces while playfully licking it off our cheeks. As we walked through the bustling promenade, listening to the carnival barkers and the children laughing all around us, Juliet perked up her ears while she listened to the announcement of the passing games. When we reached the bottle toss game, Juliet paused, grasping my arm.

"Why don't we try this one?" she said, pinching me playfully.

"You *do* realize this is the most impossible one to win?" I said, watching the contestants' plastic rings bouncing over the rows of stacked bottles and falling into the pit below. "I'm not sure those rings even *fit* over the top of these bottles..."

"Well, at least we'll have a level playing field then," she

smiled. "It can't hurt to try. Come on, let's just play one round."

"Okay," I said, paying the attendant for six rings. "Why don't you go first?"

I handed Juliet three rings and she paused, holding one of them over the retaining wall while she concentrated on her aim. She tossed the first ring in the air and it bounced noisily over the lip of one of the glass bottles.

"See?" I said, bumping her ass while I glanced at the game attendant with a frown. "I told you this was impossible."

"Don't be such a skeptic," Juliet huffed. "You have to *believe* in it to make it happen. We still have five more rings. Now it's your turn."

I leaned over the wall separating the contestants from the rows of bottles, targeting the bottle closest to my position and lofted my ring gently in the air, watching it bounce over the tops of three bottles before landing in the pit.

"Arghh," I groaned, furrowing my brow frustratingly. "Like I said earlier, I'm not even sure if these rings fit over any of these bottles. I've never seen anyone actually land one successfully."

"Maybe we just need to *concentrate* a little harder," Juliet said, holding her second ring in front of her body and grimacing when she heard it bounce over one of the bottles and fall into the pit.

I tossed my last ring, watching it bounce unsuccessfully over the top of the bottles, then Juliet hesitated, holding her third ring out in front of her as she closed her eyes.

"I'm not sure that's going to help much," I chuckled, watching the look of concentration on her face.

She slowly tossed her ring with a gentle spiral to keep it from flipping over in the air, and it landed on top of one of the bottles, circling like a spinning top for a few seconds before settling down and nesting over the neck of the flask.

"We have a winner!" the carnival attendant announced, pointing toward Juliet.

"Woo-hoo!" she squealed, jumping up and down in glee.

"What kind of prize would you like?" the attendant said, approaching the two of us and pointing up towards the row of stuffed animals hanging from the ceiling. "You qualify for a mid-sized toy."

"What do they have available?" Juliet said, turning toward me while she stared straight ahead.

"Just about everything," I said, scanning the row of plush toys. "Giraffes, teddy bears, baby elephants–"

"I'll have the *elephant*!" Juliet gushed. "Dumbo was always my favorite cartoon character when I was a kid, with his oversize ears and his adorable face. He reminded me of *myself* while I was losing my sight and learning to rely more and more on my hearing to make my way in the world."

I nodded toward the attendant, then he handed us the stuffed animal.

"Do you want me to carry it for you?" I said. "You've got enough to worry about, trying to avoid bumping into people while we make our way through this busy crowd."

"As long as you keep holding on to me," Juliet nodded, having decided to forego bringing her cane and using me as her chaperone instead. "I'm afraid I might drop him."

We continued down the main thoroughfare of the game pit, then Juliet paused again when she heard the distinctive sound of the little groundhogs popping their heads up on the popular game *Whack-a-Mole*.

"I remember playing this game as a kid," she smiled. "It was always one of my favorites."

"But how can you have a chance of *hitting* one when you can't even see them?" I said, squinting my eyes suspiciously.

"The machine makes a little sound before popping each of the moles up. If I concentrate on the sound, I have a little forewarning before deciding where to move my mallet. Why don't you give it a try first?"

"Okay," I said, handing the attendant a five-dollar bill to pay for two turns.

When I pressed the button to start the first game, I closed my eyes for a moment, trying to focus on the sound of the popping heads. But each time the machine pinged and I slammed my mallet in the direction of the sound, I came up empty. When I heard the timer signaling that my time was about to run out, I opened my eyes in frustration and slammed the hammer haphazardly over the disappearing animal heads.

"That didn't help much," I chuckled, handing Juliet the mallet for her turn. "So much for having an advantage with my eyes closed."

"Always the doubter," Juliet said, moving my hand over the start button. "Watch and learn, grasshopper."

She grasped the baton with two hands, signaling for me to start the game, then she systematically slammed the mallet over the heads of each of the bopping moles one at a time until the game time finally ran out.

"We have a perfect score!" the game attendant barked over the p.a. system, pointing toward Juliet while I gazed at her with wide eyes.

"How did you do that?" I said, shaking my head incredulously. "I've never seen *anyone* snare every mole in this game!"

"Like I said earlier," Juliet smiled. "Sometimes there's an *advantage* to relying on our other perceptions."

"So I'm beginning to see," I nodded.

"What prize would you like?" the attendant said, peering at Juliet's vacant eyes. "You can choose from any of the largest animals."

"Do they have a panda bear?" she said, turning toward me.

"A very *big* one, yes," I said, peering up at the row of stuffed toys.

"I'll take it!" she said, bobbing up and down excitedly on her tiptoes.

I wrapped my arm around the panda bear's midsection, carrying the stuffed elephant in my other arm while I led Juliet away from the game pit area.

"I'm not sure we'll be able to fit any more of these things in my car at this rate," I chuckled. "Let alone carry them through the fairgrounds for the rest of the day."

"Let's mix it up and go for a *ride* then," Juliet said. "That'll give us a chance to rest the toys while we take a little breather. Besides, I'd hate to embarrass you anymore with my special talents while playing more of the games."

"Ps-shaw!" I huffed, grabbing her arm and steering her in the direction of the midway. "Let's see how well you do on the *SuperTwister*. Something tells me your stomach won't be as strong as mine in surviving that ride."

"Not to worry, sweetheart," Juliet smiled, squeezing my hand. "I'm used to being tossed around next to you, not knowing where our ride will take us next. Bring it on!"

I purchased a ticket package for three rides at the nearest booth, then we got in line for the scariest roller coaster at the fair. When we finally walked onto the entrance ramp at the base of the paused ride, we sat side-by-side in one of the cars near the front of the column, placing the bear between the two of us and Dumbo wedged between the safety bar and her stomach.

"Are you sure you're ready for this?" I grinned, squeezing her hand as the train of carriages rattled forward and slowly started moving up the steep entrance ramp.

"No worries," she grinned, tickling the palm of my hand with her fingers. "Are *you*? Maybe you should close your eyes so you don't get frightened too much..."

"Fat chance of that," I said. "I already tried that technique and it didn't work."

"I didn't hear you complaining when you were *blindfolded* last night," she chuckled.

Suddenly, our car crested the top of the ramp and we whooshed a hundred feet straight downward while Juliet raised her arms over her head, squealing in delight as her long hair blew in the wind. While our car lurched from side to side over the winding path of the coaster at a terrifying speed, she continued holding her arms over her head the entire time, feeling the centripetal forces swaying her body while she grinned and I clasped the safety bar in front of me with white knuckles. When the ride finally lurched to a stop at the bottom of the ramp, I stumbled out of our carriage, walking dizzily onto the platform.

"Whoa, girl," Juliet said, grabbing hold of my arm as I tried to balance the two stuffed animals in each of my arms. "Maybe we should try something a little slower for our next ride."

"Good idea," I said, peering up at the large, slowly revolving wheel at the end of the midway. "How about the Ferris wheel?"

"Okay," Juliet said, interlacing her arm between mine. "At least we won't have to worry about our furry friends flying out of the ride this time."

We waited in line for the start of the next ride and when the attendant locked the door to our private gondola behind us and we began to feel the wheel slowly turning upward, I sighed a breath of relief.

"This is much more relaxing," I said. "You were right about that last one. I much prefer tossing around in *bed* with you than on that roller coaster."

"Yes," Juliet nodded. "But this one is kind of boring. There's nothing to keep me stimulated. At least you can peer down over the fairgrounds to distract your attention. I've got nothing to keep me distracted beyond the gentle rocking of our carriage."

"Perhaps you'd like me to rock something *else* to keep you stimulated while we're locked in this thing?" I smiled, pressing my hand between her thighs over her tight-fitting jeans.

"Do you think we have enough *time*?" Juliet said, slowly parting her legs.

"I suppose that depends on you," I smiled. "But instead of going slow and gentle, we might have to work a little faster this time."

"What did you have in mind, exactly?" Juliet said, squirming her ass while I gently probed her warm crotch. "I'm not sure I want to get naked on this seat that a million people have sat on."

"Maybe we don't have to," I grinned, pulling down the zipper of her jeans. "Why don't I keep a lookout while I finger you down the front of your pants?"

"Mmm," Juliet hummed, moaning softly as the tips of my fingers inched toward her moist pussy. "If you insist. That might make this ride a little more interesting..."

I pushed my hand lower under the front of her jeans, lubricating my fingers in her dripping slit, then I slowly pulled them back, circling her clit with my slippery digits. Juliet titled her head back and rested it on the cushion of our seat, spreading her legs further apart as I began to massage her gland more vigorously.

"Better?" I said, watching her roll her hips as I fingered her pussy.

"Much," she panted, parting her lips while she groaned more loudly. "How much more time have we got?"

I peered outside our carriage for a moment, noticing our gondola nearing the top of the wheel, pressing my middle fingers deeper inside her slit.

"About halfway. Do you think you can come from me just *fingering* you?"

"If you keep doing it *that* way," she grunted, tilting her hips upward to sink my digits even further in her hole. "Rub your palm against my clit while you finger me inside."

I paused for a moment, remembering the instructions of our coach when I attended a women's sex workshop where a group of us learned how to squirt. The trick, I learned, was to gradually stimulate the G-spot a few inches inside the top edge of the vagina while relaxing the sphincter muscles to allow the Skene's gland containing our ejaculatory fluid to express itself when we climaxed. As I began to press more firmly on the upper surface of her cavity while gently massaging her bulging gland, Juliet groaned and rocked her hips more vigorously.

"That feels heavenly," she grunted. "Whatever you're doing, you're giving me a whole different kind of feeling. It almost feels like I have to *pee.*"

"It won't be pee if you relax your muscles properly," I said. "This is something I learned at a special sex workshop for women. When you stimulate the gland nestled behind this spot in your pussy, you make your G-spot swell and prepare to release a special fluid that makes women squirt–"

"Like the way *you* did yesterday?" Juliet panted, beginning to rock her hips more rapidly.

"Yes," I said, pressing my fingers harder against her swelling bump and feeling the inside of her pussy expanding in preparation for a powerful contraction.

"Are you sure I'm not going to wet my pants?" she hissed, tightening her jaw muscles as her whole body began to tense up.

"Not with *urine*," I smiled, watching a deep flush roll over the top of her neck and onto her cheeks. "Just let it go, baby. You'll find it makes your orgasm even more powerful and intense. Gush all over my hands."

"Oh God," she huffed, raising her hips off the seat. "Here it comes, I can't stop it now. Oh fuck–I'm *comingggg*!"

I peered down and watched Juliet's hips shaking while she sprayed her juices all over my hand, creating a giant wet spot in the front of her jeans. As our carriage neared the bottom of the circle and our wheel slowed to a stop, I quickly pulled up her zipper while Juliet prepared to exit the ride.

"Here," I said, handing her the big panda resting on the seat beside me. "Maybe *you* should carry this for a while now. You've made quite a mess of yourself, and we don't want people wondering what happened to you."

"I just had my first female *ejaculation*, is what happened to me," she grinned, still breathing heavily as she exited the gondola, clasping the stuffed toy tightly over her stomach. "I wouldn't mind going to one of those women's workshops sometime. I feel like I'm just scratching the surface of possibilities for intimate relations between women..."

"We could do that," I smiled, leading her down the ramp

toward the exit of the fairgrounds. "Or you could let *me* teach you instead. After all, I've had a bit more experience in these things than you have."

"Works for me," Juliet smiled. "Let's get out of here. I want to feel your beautiful body crawling over me instead of all these jostling fairgoers. I've been dreaming of a few extra techniques I want to try out on you."

"Mmm," I said. "It sounds *delicious*. Do you want to stop somewhere for a bite to eat first? We might need to stock up our energy before making love again all night."

"Sure, but not here with all this greasy food. Why don't we go somewhere quiet and enjoy a relaxing gourmet meal?"

Suddenly I felt my stomach rumbling, realizing we hadn't eaten since breakfast earlier in the day.

"Okay," I nodded. "Since you cooked for me last night, it'll be my treat today. I know a nice spot not far from your place that serves the freshest fish and desserts to die for."

"I only want *you* for dessert," Juliet purred, clasping my hand more tightly as we headed through the parking lot back toward my car.

"I think that can be arranged," I smiled. "If it's anything like *last* night's after-dinner treat, I can't wait..."

10

After our exciting adventure at the county fair, we drove to one of my favorite restaurants near the waterfront and I parked the car, leading her into the sumptuous dining room of *Oriole,* with its huge floor-to-ceiling views of the lake.

"You should like this place," I smiled when the maître d' greeted us at the front desk. "It reminds me of your apartment. Can you smell the aroma of the lakefront?"

"Yes," Juliet nodded. "Plus, I heard the seagulls as soon as we got out of the car. Do they serve seafood here?"

"Absolutely," the maître d' said, overhearing our conversation. "We have a broad selection of seafood from our Michelin-star-awarded chef. Would you like a table near the window?"

"Maybe something a little more private near the corner of the room," I said, concerned about the other patrons staring at Juliet.

"As you wish," the headwaiter said. "Please follow me."

He led us to a small table near the fall wall, and when we sat down in the plush chairs, Juliet brushed her fingers over the bottom of the linen tablecloths draped over the side of our table.

"*Fancy*," she said.

"Only the best for my girl," I smiled.

"Can I start you off with something to drink?" the maître d' said.

"I'll have a cosmopolitan," I nodded.

"Sex on the beach for me please," Juliet said nonchalantly.

"Coming right up," the maître d' said, departing in the direction of the bar.

"Haven't you had *enough* for one day?" I smirked, kicking her gently under the table.

"*Never*," she grinned, sliding her foot sensuously up the side of my calf.

When our waiter returned with our drinks, I ordered the potato-crusted halibut and Juliet ordered the maple-glazed salmon for the main courses, then we sipped our cocktails for a while, listening to the sound of the boats and the gulls cruising about the pier.

"Did you enjoy our little outing at the fair?" I said, happy that the long tablecloths concealed the dark stain on the front of her jeans.

"Yes," she smiled, taking a deep gulp of her cocktail. "Though I'm not sure which I enjoyed more, whupping your ass at the game tables or coming all over your hand in the privacy of our own booth on the Ferris wheel."

"I certainly know which one *I* did," I grinned, caressing her foot under the table. "Though I'm intrigued about something you said before we left. You said you were dreaming about some other techniques you wanted to try out on me. What exactly were you thinking?"

"Well," Juliet said, kicking off her sneakers under the

table and sliding her foot up the inside of my leg. "I was thinking of doing this with you in the bathtub at home, but it looks like we'll have plenty enough privacy to do it right here..."

"Do *what* exactly?" I said, peering around me to see if anyone was looking while she lifted her foot higher between my legs and pressed her toes between my thighs.

"I've been dreaming about fucking you with my *toes*," she smiled. "It's something I heard about in another one of my favorite audiobooks, and I've always wanted to try it."

"Right *here*?" I said, widening my eyes.

"Why not?" she said. "Do you think you'll be able to keep your moans to a dull roar so you don't distract the attention of the other diners? We've got plenty of cover under the table from the draped tablecloths."

"I'm not sure," I grunted, feeling her toes curling over the front of my crotch. "But at least I've got a layer of protection to help dull the sensation–"

"What's the fun in that?" Juliet said, flapping her toes over my moistening pussy. "Besides, if you keep your jeans on while I do this, you're just likely to get another embarrassing stain in your pants. And this time, we won't have the protection of a large stuffed animal to conceal it from the other onlookers."

"You want me to take my *pants* off under the table?" I said, flaring my eyes open.

"Discreetly, yes," Juliet nodded. "I'm guessing most of the other patrons are staring out the window instead of looking at us sheltered in this corner of the room."

I glanced around me again, noticing the other diners chatting quietly amongst themselves, occasionally peering out the large picture windows. I was happy they had a diversion from staring at the blind girl who was staring straight ahead while she talked to me, but I was even happier that we had a modicum of privacy to carry out our little crime of passion.

"Yes," I said, slipping my hands under the bottom of the tablecloth and shimmying my jeans and panties down over my ankles. I could feel the soft velvet of the plush seats caressing my bare pussy, and I worried about leaving a different kind of stain on the upholstery by the time we finished our illicit affair.

When the waiter returned with our main courses and placed them gently in front of our place settings, I was happy for the distraction while I glanced up at him coolly.

"Can I get you anything else?" he said, peering at our flushed faces.

"No thank you," I said, feeling my pussy buzzing under the table while Juliet tapped her toes playfully against my dripping slit. "I think we've got everything we need right here."

"No kidding," Juliet said after the waiter left our table. "How does that Shakespeare line go? All I need is a loaf of bread, a jug of wine, and thou?"

"I think it was *Omar Khayyam* actually, but close enough," I grunted as Juliet slid her toes over my throbbing clit.

"Mmm, you feel *delicious*," Juliet said, picking up her silverware and beginning to eat her entrée while she stimulated me with her foot.

"Are you going to eat your *food* while you fuck me under the table?" I said, groaning softly as I tilted my hips upward to press my pussy harder against her foot.

"Why not?" Juliet grinned. "You should do it too, otherwise people might become suspicious of why we're watching our gourmet food growing cold."

"That might be easier for *you* than for me," I chuckled, picking up my cutlery and cutting a shaky slice of my halibut.

But as soon as I placed the first mouthful in my mouth, Juliet abruptly lowered her foot, thrusting her big toe into my hole. I choked for a moment on my food then I raised my napkin to my face to distract the diners' sudden attention, feeling my eyes watering from the rising pleasure washing over me.

"Are you okay over there?" Juliet said, grinning like a Cheshire Cat. "Maybe you should have a glass of water or something."

"I'm fine, miss smartypants," I said, clearing my throat. "At least I *was*, until you stuck your toe in my pussy."

"You don't *like* it?" she grinned back at me. "Do you want me to stop?"

"God no," I grunted, beginning to rock my hips in unison with the thrusting movement of her toe. "I haven't had this much fun since, well, since we had sex in *another* public place."

"Where the whole time I was thinking about how soon I could *return* the favor," she smiled.

"It seems your wish has come true," I groaned, closing my eyes while I felt the pleasure rising inside me. "If you keep doing that, I'm going to make an entirely *different* kind of mess."

"Oh?" Juliet said, redoubling her effort under the table while she flexed her toe inside my slit, tilting it upwards toward my bulging G-spot. "Am I stimulating the right area to make you gush and squirt again? I'm dying to see what that feels like on my bare foot."

"I don't think you have anything to worry about," I panted, feeling myself rapidly approaching the point of no return. "It doesn't take much to set me off..."

"*Come*, baby," Juliet purred, staring straight into my eyes while I peered back at her with dilated pupils. "Come for me in front of all these fancy restaurant patrons while I feel your pussy pulsing against my foot."

"Oh God," I huffed, scrunching the sides of the tablecloth beside me in my clenched hands while I tried to maintain my composure. "I can't stop it now–"

When my climax finally washed over me, I clamped my thighs tightly over Juliet's probing foot, gushing my juices hard all over the bottom of her leg and the now-drenched seat, unable to restrain myself from making a loud grunting sound while I quivered in my chair. When I noticed a few heads turning in my direction, I picked up another forkful of my sea bass, shoveling it into my mouth and humming loudly while I closed my eyes, pretending to enjoy the taste of the food instead of the strong contractions emanating from my squirting pussy under the table.

"Oh, that's *sooo* good," I fawned, putting on the performance of my life while I tried to divert everyone's attention from what was going on under the table. "This is the best sea bass I've tasted in *ages*!"

"And that's the hottest *sex* I've had in ages," Juliet whispered back at me, holding her tensed leg hard against my dripping crotch until my contractions finally stopped and I relaxed my tensing buttock muscles. "I'm starting to *like* this business of having sex in public."

I glanced nervously around the room to make sure no one had sensed what we were doing, then I noticed a lone diner three tables away staring blankly straight ahead while she held a forkful of food in mid-air a few inches from her gaping mouth. I recognized the vacant expression of another blind woman, with her head turned slightly askance as she listened intently to the unusual sounds coming from our side of the room.

"I have a feeling you're not the *only* one," I said, rustling my dinnerware noisily on my plate to divert everyone's attention back to the business at hand. "We seem to have attracted the attention of one pretty patron in particular."

"Oh?" Juliet said, retracting her foot slowly from my dripping pussy and wiping it on the lower half of her other leg. "Do you think she suspected what we were doing under the table?"

"Well, she looks to be *blind*, so I have a feeling her sense of hearing was more attuned than the others to the noises we were making over here."

"Is she alone?" Juliet said. "Maybe we should ask her to join us. Perhaps she'd like to join our little tete-a-tete?"

"That might be a little premature," I chuckled. "Besides, two blind girls eating at the same table might invite more scrutiny than we wanted."

"Yeah, especially if we're *playing* with each other under the table," Juliet grinned.

"She *does* seem intrigued, though," I said, glancing at the other girl out of the corner of my eye while she continued eating her meal and pretending to ignore our conversation as she perked up her ears. "And she's quite pretty. Maybe we can introduce ourselves and invite her to join us for dessert."

"Yes," Juliet said while she slid her sneaker back onto her foot with her other free foot. "Dessert with another pretty girl sounds like a real treat. Have you ever had sex with *three* women at the same time?"

"Maybe once or twice," I grinned.

"That sounds like something *else* you can teach me," Juliet nodded. "I'm tired of just reading about all these wild and sexy escapades. I'm ready to try it in the real world..."

11

———

After we finished our entrees, Juliet got up from our table and followed my instructions to the other girl's table, pausing by her chair as she introduced herself.

"Excuse me," she said. "I'm sorry to interrupt your dinner, but my friend couldn't help noticing that you're visually impaired, like me. "Would you like to join us for the remainder of your meal? We'd love some extra company, plus I rarely have a chance to socialize with other sightless people..."

"Um, okay," the girl said. "Can you help me carry the rest of my food to your table? I don't want to drop it on the other diners."

"Of course," Juliet said, motioning for the maître d' to assist them.

He brought an extra chair to our table and pulled out the seat for the other blind girl, positioning her kitty-corner, between me and Juliet.

"My name's Juliet, by the way," Juliet said, reaching out her hand over the tablecloth and squeezing the other girl's hand. "And this is my friend, Jade."

I reached out my hand as Juliet had and softly tapped the other girl's fingers.

"Nice to meet you," the new girl said. "My name's Skye. Thank you for inviting me to your table. I was feeling a bit lonely over there all by myself."

"Do you go out to fancy restaurants alone very *often*?" Juliet asked.

"Every now and then," Skye nodded. "It's nice to get out of the house from time to time and mingle with some real people. Plus, I get some of my best cooking ideas for new dishes at places like this."

"That's very clever," Juliet said. "I was just thinking that I'll have to try preparing this maple-glazed salmon that I've been enjoying tonight for my next home-cooked meal."

"Yes," Skye smiled. "You seemed to be enjoying your dinner more than the *rest* of the restaurant diners."

"Oh, that wasn't me," Juliet grinned, motioning in my direction. "That was *Jade*, who seemed to enjoy her dish far more than I was."

"I have a feeling that she was enjoying more than just the *food*," Skye chuckled. "Either that, or that must have been one especially juicy and succulent dish."

"Well, it certainly was *juicy*," I said. "I'm afraid I made a bit of a mess on my chair."

"Mm-hmm," Skye nodded, raising her foot over the edge of my seat. "Although that scent doesn't smell like any dish I've tried lately. At least not of the *culinary* variety."

"You're very perceptive," I chuckled. "We were hoping to keep our shenanigans under the radar before you arrived."

"Your secret is safe with me," Skye smiled. "As long as you allow me to participate in the fun and games."

"I like the sound of that," Juliet said. "But we might be

able to enjoy our second course more openly back at my place. Would you like to join us for some brandy or liqueur in a more comfortable environment?"

"I'd like that very much," Skye nodded. "I might enjoy it even more if I can *lick* it off your naked bodies."

"Oh God," Juliet grunted. "That's *one* technique I never even imagined. You're making me build up a whole new kind of appetite..."

∾

The three of us quickly paid for our meals, then we quickly left the restaurant, driving as fast as we could through the busy traffic back to Juliet's apartment. When we entered her foyer and removed our coats, we wasted little time falling into each other's arms, kissing and groping one another as we stumbled our way toward Juliet's bedroom. When we reached her bed, I began to remove Skye's clothing, running my eyes shamelessly over her full figure, much more voluptuous than Juliet's petit ballerina form. While I unclasped the back of her underwire bra with one hand, I unzipped the front of her pants, surprised to see that her bush had been neatly trimmed and shaved to a shallow stubble.

"You seem to have some experience undressing women, Jade," she said, stepping out of her pants while I lowered her underwear over her ankles.

"I've been getting a bit more practice than *usual*, lately," I nodded, watching Juliet step behind Skye and circle her hands over the blind girl's breasts, squeezing them softly.

"Lucky you," Skye moaned, arching her back as her nipples began to harden from Juliet's ministrations. "It's been longer than planned for me. Having two women at the same time is a special treat."

"Speaking of," Juliet said, temporarily halting her exploration of Skye's naked body. "I've completely forgotten about our after-dinner drinks. Would you like to repair to the kitchen while I prepare some digestifs?"

"Maybe later," Skye said, turning around and rubbing her tits against Juliet's naked body while I caressed her ass and slipped my finger under her moist slit. "I'd hate to interrupt a good thing right now. I love your figure, you're so firm and petite. I like petite girls–"

"Are you *lesbian*?" Juliet said, groaning softly while Skye pressed her tongue into her mouth and slipped her hand between her legs.

"For as long as I can remember," Skye nodded. "Boys seem to have an aversion to blind girls. But I've enjoyed being with women ever since my juvenile sleepover days. Plus, they're a little easier to *decipher*, since their bodies are similar to mine..."

"I wouldn't be so sure about that," Juliet said, sliding the palms of her hands over the edges of Skye's flared hips and under the curvature of her plump ass. You seem to be built more like Jennifer Lopez than Alicia Vikander..."

"How would you know if you're blind?" Skye said, squinting her brows.

"I wasn't born blind," Juliet said. "I had a little time to enjoy a few American movies before I lost my sight. Those were two of my favorite actresses."

"Same here," Skye said, grinding her bristly mound against Juliet's furry muff while I caressed their slits from behind. "I'd happily fuck either one of them."

"*Speaking* of which," Juliet said, pulling a few inches away to invite me to join in the action. "How are we going to do this with three women? I'm not as experienced as the two of you."

"I'm happy just to *watch* for a while," I said, caressing the two women's hardening nipples as they continued groping one another. "I have a feeling that Skye knows her way around a woman's body. Maybe I can pick up a few extra tips studying her technique."

"I like the sound of that," Skye nodded, grabbing hold of Juliet's hand and pushing her down over the surface of the bed.

She climbed on top of Juliet, rolling her slippery pussy over her tits and down the middle of her stomach while leaving a trail of glistening juices over her abdomen, grinding her pussy on Juliet's bush and soaking it thoroughly. I chose to sit on the foot of the bed, watching the two women making love, not wanting to interrupt the new girl's mojo. The two blind girls seemed to be innately drawn to one another, and I became increasingly aroused while fingering myself, watching them writhing their bodies together.

While Juliet groaned from Skye's expert caresses, the new girl angled Juliet's body to the side, pushing her legs apart and raising one over her shoulder. Then she spread her knees apart and squatted between Julie's legs, sliding her dripping pussy between Juliet's thighs and pressing their cunts together. Although I'd scissored Juliet similarly the previous night, it was obvious to me that Skye had done this many times before in the superior position. She seemed much more comfortable playing the top position in the relationship, preferring her partner to play the submissive femme role.

While she proceeded to grind her glistening vulva over Juliet's equally wet pussy, I watched Juliet's face from the back of the bed, noticing her growing comfortable in the role, perfectly happy to let Skye take the lead while she groaned and squeezed Skye's oversize tits. It was tempting for me to try to slide in on the action as I watched their slurping pussies grinding together and Skye's full tits bouncing up and down, but I thought I should leave the two blind women to their own devices to enjoy the rare opportunity of savoring their unique experience together. It didn't take long for their movements to begin escalating in intensity, and I looked on with a mixture of jealousy and lustfulness as their hips began to shake together while they wailed at the peak of their passion. After they finished climaxing together, Skye flopped down onto the bed beside Juliet, kissing her gently as she caressed her trembling stomach.

"You've been awfully quiet over there, Jade," Juliet said, lifting her head in my direction. "It's not like you to sit alone on the sidelines. Don't you want a piece of the action?"

"I dunno," I smiled halfheartedly. "Skye seems to have things well in hand. Plus, I already had my fill over dinner from your expert toes."

"I'm sure we could fit you into the puzzle somehow," Juliet smiled. "If it feels this good for two women to have sex together, it has to be even better with *three* of us doing it at the same time."

"I suppose that's up to our *guest*," I said, still feeling self-conscious about the intrusion of the new girl into our relationship. "She hasn't had as much experience making love to you as I have. Plus, it looks like she's still exploring your body..."

"Mmm," Juliet grunted as Skye inserted two fingers deep into her dripping pussy. "But I've still got my *top* half free. Why don't you sit on my face and let me lick your pussy while Skye has her way with my lower half? Maybe you can watch her from the other side this time and soak up her body while she makes love to me a different way."

"That's okay with *me* if that works for Skye," I said, peering at the other girl with a curious expression.

"Sure," Skye nodded, happy to keep a measure of distance between the two of us while she continued to stimulate Juliet in her own way. "This time, I want to *taste* your pussy while I watch you come."

"That makes *two* of us," Juliet smiled. "Why don't you watch me licking Jade's cunny while you go down on me, then we can switch turns the next time around?"

"Okay," Skye said, sounding unconvinced.

It seemed more and more apparent the more time the three of us spent time together that Skye wanted Juliet all to herself, and for her part, Juliet seemed equally happy to let her have her way with her. While Skye shimmied her way down Juliet's body and planted her face between her legs, I slowly climbed atop Juliet's face, straddling her rosebud lips with my trembling pussy. She peered up at my glistening folds and smelled my musky scent, smiling at me.

"Don't be shy *now*, Jade," she said, grabbing hold of the sides of my ass and guiding my hips down over her waiting lips. "I've wanted to feel you gushing over my face again ever since last night. Maybe watching Skye lick me at the same time will make you even more turned on. I can't wait to feel you spraying all over my neck and tits."

"Okay..." I murmured, watching Skye slide her tongue expertly over Juliet's dripping folds as she teased and tormented her.

While Juliet began sucking my hardening clit into her mouth, I watched Skye's technique and Juliet's response from the movement of her hips, becoming more and more aroused by the erotic stimulation from both sides. But there was something about the way Skye touched Juliet that had me mesmerized. Whether it was because the two women felt a unique connection from both being blind, or because Skye had plenty of experience with prior women, I wasn't sure. But the growing bond between them was becoming increasingly obvious to me, and although Juliet was trying her best to give me expert head, there was something that was holding me back from fully enjoying the experience.

As Juliet's hips began to rock more excitedly from Skye's unique form of stimulation and her moans from under my hips began to grow more animated, I gradually became more aroused, knowing she was getting close to another orgasm. When she finally climaxed with Skye's face deeply embedded between her legs, I had a brief, unconscious climax, more out of sympathy with what Juliet was feeling than from the soft caresses of her tongue. When we both finished climaxing, I lifted my hips off Juliet's face and she peered up at me with a curious expression.

"You didn't *squirt* this time," she said. "Should I have been using my *finger* to stimulate you at the same time? Your orgasm didn't seem as strong as usual–"

"No," I lied. "I enjoyed feeling your tongue as much as ever. I was just a bit distracted watching Skye going down on you and watching your body responding to her touch."

"Yeah," Juliet smiled when Skye shifted her body back up the bed and lay down beside her. "That was pretty incredible. Skye seems to be just as experienced making love to women as you are."

I paused for a moment, watching the two blind women caressing one another intuitively.

"You two seem to have an extra connection that I can't duplicate. It's quite lovely to see, actually," I said, feeling my heart sinking.

"Well, we'll have plenty of time for more of this *tomorrow*," Juliet said. "I'm in no hurry to see either of you leave. Will you both spend the night with me and stick around for some more fun and games tomorrow?"

"I'd love to," Skye said, snuggling up closer to Juliet and wrapping her legs around her hips, as if claiming her for herself.

"Of course," I said, feeling increasingly like the odd women out. "Like you said, three is better than two..."

I pulled the blanket over the three of us and nuzzled my nose into the side of Juliet's neck while Skye draped an arm over her midsection, carefully avoiding touching my body. It didn't take long for the two of them to fall asleep and while I listened to them breathing peacefully side-by-side, I knew what I had to do. I shimmied out of bed slowly, pretending to go pee in the washroom, then I got dressed quietly in the other room, preparing to leave the apartment. But I didn't want to leave Juliet wondering why I'd left without an expla- nation, so I pulled out my phone and typed her a short text message, knowing she'd be able to listen to the audio version when she woke up in the morning.

Dear Juliet,

It's been a singular pleasure getting to know you these past couple of days. I haven't had so much fun with another person for as long as I can remember. I'll never forget the special bond that we shared and the fun times we had at the fair, in the restaurant, and of course at home with you in your beautiful apartment.

But after seeing you with Skye, it's obvious she can give you something I never can. You two have an affinity that transcends more than just sightlessness, and you belong together. Besides, I've always been a restless soul, and I'd hate for the two of us to

*develop stronger feelings for one another, only to be pulled apart
sometime in the future.*

Wishing you and Skye all the best,

Love, Jade

After pressing the send button on my phone, I opened the front door and closed it quietly behind me, shedding a lone tear down the front of my face while I stepped into the elevator taking me down to the ground floor. This was one short-term fling I'd never forget, but I knew that Juliet was in better hands with another blind woman. While I headed toward my car parked on the side of the street, I closed my eyes listening to the sound of the gulls circling over the waterfront and smelling the moist air drifting in from the lake, smiling at how the pretty blind girl had opened my eyes to a whole new world of sensations and pleasures.

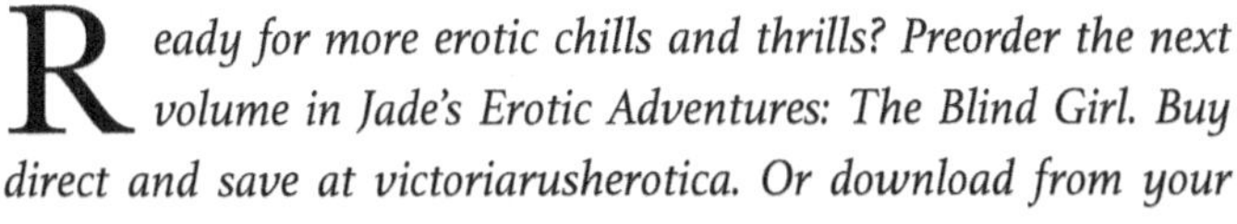

Ready for more erotic chills and thrills? Preorder the next volume in Jade's Erotic Adventures: *The Blind Girl*. Buy direct and save at victoriarusherotica. Or download from your favorite online bookstore here: retailer links.

*When she becomes lost in Amish Country, Jade opens more
than just the eyes of a sheltered farm girl..*

ALSO BY VICTORIA RUSH

Adult Fairytales:

The Enchanted Forest: An Erotic Fairytale

The Land of Giants: An Erotic Fairytale

The Dragon's Lair: An Erotic Fairytale

Witch's Brew: An Erotic Fairytale

The Mage's Spell: An Erotic Fairytale

The Mermaid Lagoon: An Erotic Fairytale

The Coven: An Erotic Fairytale

Rapunzel: An Erotic Fairytale

The Seven Dwarfs: An Erotic Fairytale

The Land of Mutants: An Erotic Fairytale

The Erotic Temple: A Sexy Fairytale (Coming Soon)

Erotica Themed Bundles:

Voyeur: Lesbian Erotica Bundle

Public Affairs: A Lesbian Anthology

Futa Fantasies: The Ladyboy Collection

Threesomes: The Lesbian Collection

Threesomes - Volume 2: The Lesbian Collection

First Time: A Lesbian Anthology

Hedonism: An Erotic Anthology

Switch Hitters: Bisexual Erotica

Taboo Erotica: The Lesbian Series

BDSM: The Lesbian Collection

Party Games: The Erotic Collection

Party Games 2: The Erotic Collection

All Girl 1: Lesbian Erotica Bundle

All Girl 2: Lesbian Erotica Bundle

All Girl 3: Lesbian Erotica Bundle

All Girl 4: Lesbian Erotica Bundle

Erotic Fairytale Bundles:

Clover's Fantasy Adventures: Books 1 - 5

Clover's Fantasy Adventures: Books 6 - 10

Erotic Fantasy:

Pirate's Bounty: A Time Travel Adventure

Wild West: A Time Travel Adventure

Private Riley: A Time Travel Adventure

Cleopatra's Secret: A Time Travel Adventure

Bounty Hunter 2125: A Time Travel Adventure

Ninja Assassin: A Time Travel Adventure

The 300: A Time Travel Adventure

Arabian Nights: An Erotic Fairytale (coming soon...)

Steamy Time Travel Bundles:

Riley's Time Travel Adventures: Books 1 - 5

Lesbian Erotica:

The Dinner Party: Lesbian Voyeur Erotica

The Darkroom: Bisexual Voyeur Erotica

Naked Yoga: Lesbian Transgender Erotica

Nude Cruise: Bisexual Voyeur Erotica

Rush Hour: Taboo Public Sex

The Girl Next Door: First Time Lesbian Erotic Romance

Girls' Camp: Lesbian Group Sex

Wet Dream: Ladyboy Fantasy Erotica

The Convent: Taboo Sex with a Nun

Sex Robot: A Dream Sex Machine

The Personal Trainer: Getting Pumped at the Gym

The Dominatrix: BDSM Lesbian Domination

Webcam Chat: Lesbian Online Sex

Paint Me: A Kinky Bodypainting Workshop

The Toy Party: Girls Sharing Sex Toys

The Costume Party: Strapping One On

Swedish Sauna: Lesbian Group Sex

The Therapist: Taboo Lesbian Erotica

Elevator Shaft: Bisexual Threesomes Erotica

Ladyboy: Lesbian Transgender Erotica

Peep Show: Lesbian Voyeur Erotica

The Dare: Public Sex Erotica

Maid Service: Lesbian Threesomes Erotica

The Hitchhiker: First Time Lesbian Erotica

The Housesitter: Spycam Lesbian Erotica

The Spa: Lesbian Group Orgy

Parlor Games: Blindfold Sex Party

The Exchange Student: First Time Lesbian Erotica

The Hostel: Bisexual Group Erotica

The Harem: Lesbian Erotic Romance

The Orient Express: Lesbian Voyeur Erotica

The First Lady: A Forbidden Lesbian Erotic Romance

The Slave: Lesbian BDSM Erotica

The Masseuse: Lesbian Sensuous Erotica

Too Close for Comfort: Lesbian Forbidden Erotica

Naked Twister: A Wild Party Game

Lexi: The Sex App (Lesbian Fantasy Erotica)

Call Girl: Lesbian Bisexual Threesomes Erotica

Circle Jill: Lesbian Masturbation Workshop

The Viewing Room: Masturbation Voyeur Erotica

Spin the Bottle: A Kinky Party Game

The Hair Salon: Lesbian Voyeur Erotica

Tribadism 1: Girls Only Sex Workshop

Tribadism 2: The Art of Scissoring

Tribadism 3: Threeway Hookups

The Kiss: A Game of Oral Sex

Pledge Week: Sorority Sisters

Carny Games 1: A Wild Sex Party

Carny Games 2: A Kinky Sex Party

Carny Games 3: An Erotic Sex Party

Dreamscape: An Artificial Reality Game

Glory Hole: Guess Who's On the Other Side

Joy Ride: A Late Night Erotic Bus Trip

The Blind Girl: An Erotic Romance(Coming Soon)

Lesbian Erotica Bundles:

Jade's Erotic Adventures: Books 1 - 5

Jade's Erotic Adventures: Books 6 - 10

Jade's Erotic Adventures: Books 11 - 15

Jade's Erotic Adventures: Books 16 - 20

Jade's Erotic Adventures: Books 21 - 25

Jade's Erotic Adventures: Books 26 - 30

Jade's Erotic Adventures: Books 31 - 35

Jade's Erotic Adventures: Books 36 - 40

Jade's Erotic Adventures: Books 41 - 45

Jade's Erotic Adventures: Books 46 - 50

Fifty Shades of Jade: Superbundle

Standalone Stories:

The Polynesian Girl: A Lesbian EroticRomance

FOLLOW VICTORIA RUSH:

Want to keep informed of my latest erotic book releases? Sign up for my newsletter and receive a FREE bonus book:

Spying on the neighbors just got a lot more interesting...